Pussycats
Everywhere!

For Bounder,
who went exploring for twenty-three days
and came home thinner, but wiser.

A Firefly Book

Published by Firefly Books Ltd. 2000

First Printing

U.S. Cataloging-in-Publication Data is available.

Canadian Cataloguing in Publication Data

McGraw, Sheila
    Pussycats everywhere!

ISBN 1-55209-346-8 (bound) ISBN 1-55209-348-4 (pbk.)

I. Title.

PS8575.G78P87 2000   jC813'.54   C00-930872-5
PZ7.M337Pu 2000

Published in Canada in 2000 by
Firefly Books Ltd.
3680 Victoria Park Avenue
Willowdale, Ontario, Canada   M2H 3K1

Published in the United States in 2000 by
Firefly Books (U.S.) Inc.
P.O. Box 1338, Ellicott Station
Buffalo, New York 14205

Printed and bound in Canada by Friesens, Altona, Manitoba

The Publisher acknowledges the financial support of the Government of Canada through the Book Publishing Industry Development Program for its publishing activities.

Pussycats Everywhere!

BY SHEILA McGRAW

FIREFLY BOOKS

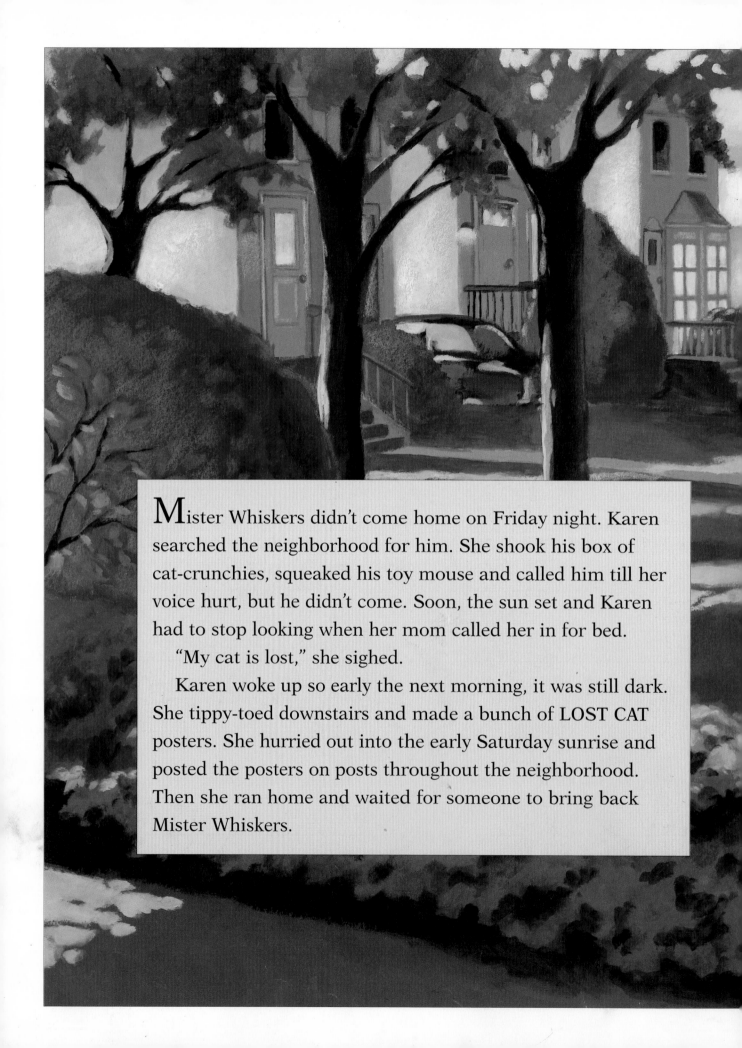

Mister Whiskers didn't come home on Friday night. Karen searched the neighborhood for him. She shook his box of cat-crunchies, squeaked his toy mouse and called him till her voice hurt, but he didn't come. Soon, the sun set and Karen had to stop looking when her mom called her in for bed.

"My cat is lost," she sighed.

Karen woke up so early the next morning, it was still dark. She tippy-toed downstairs and made a bunch of LOST CAT posters. She hurried out into the early Saturday sunrise and posted the posters on posts throughout the neighborhood. Then she ran home and waited for someone to bring back Mister Whiskers.

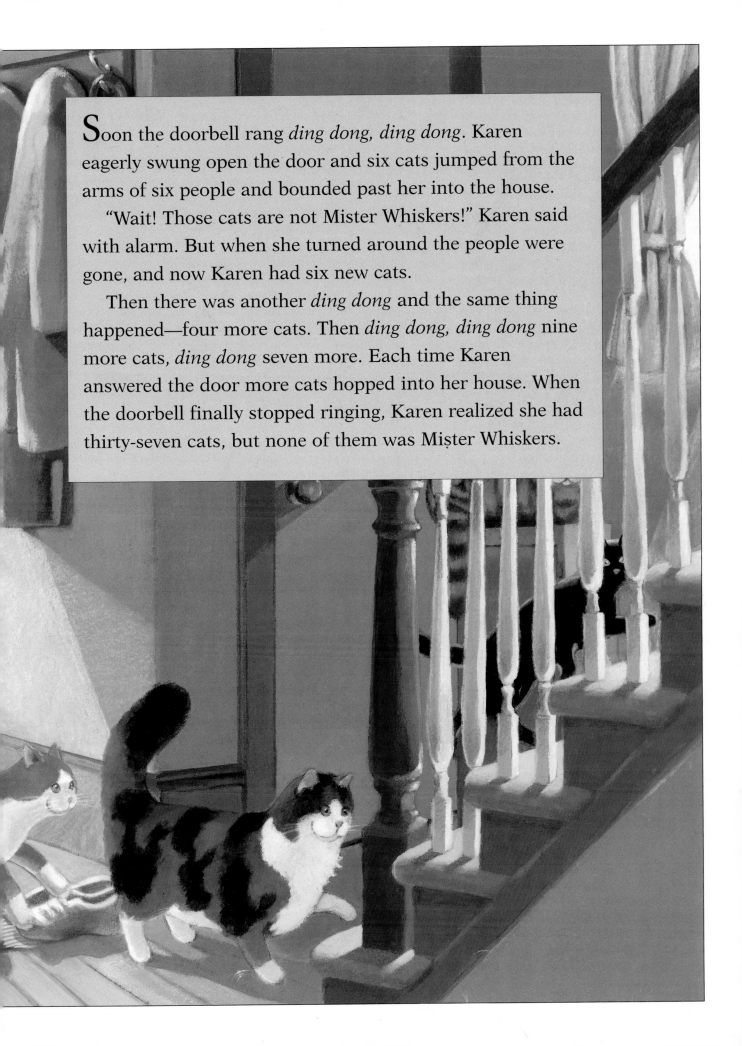

Soon the doorbell rang *ding dong, ding dong*. Karen eagerly swung open the door and six cats jumped from the arms of six people and bounded past her into the house.

"Wait! Those cats are not Mister Whiskers!" Karen said with alarm. But when she turned around the people were gone, and now Karen had six new cats.

Then there was another *ding dong* and the same thing happened—four more cats. Then *ding dong, ding dong* nine more cats, *ding dong* seven more. Each time Karen answered the door more cats hopped into her house. When the doorbell finally stopped ringing, Karen realized she had thirty-seven cats, but none of them was Mister Whiskers.

The *ding donging*, meowing, door opening, door closing and purring woke up Karen's mom and dad and they came downstairs to see what all the racket was about. When Mom and Dad saw the thirty-seven cats their eyes grew enormous and they both exclaimed, "Pussycats everywhere!"

Karen looked around. Her parents were right, there were pussycats everywhere. It was like they were up to their knees in a pond of cats.

"But no Mister Whiskers," said Karen sadly. Mom and Dad quickly got over their surprise and patted the cats and scratched behind their ears, which cats like very, very much.

Karen showed her parents one of the LOST CAT posters.

"Uh oh, I think I see how we got all these kitties," Dad said with a laugh. "Your poster doesn't say what Mr. Whiskers looks like, so those people brought the wrong cats. What will we do with a zillion-trillion cats?"

"Not a zillion-trillion Daddy, just thirty-seven," said Karen, as she dished out bowls of cat food.

"Don't forget to give them some water," said Mom with a little smile. And Karen knew right then that they'd look after the lost cats, at least for a while.

When the cats had finished eating, some went off to find a cozy spot, or a sunbeam, for catnapping. Karen stroked their soft furry tummies, scratched under their chins and behind their ears. She rubbed their velvety faces and cuddled those sleepy purring cats.

Then she went to see what the wide-awake ones were up to.

For the rest of the day the cats kept Karen busy. They helped Karen with her homework and they helped Dad with the laundry.

Karen rescued Goldie the fish, Ratboy
the hamster, china plates, flowering
plants and family treasures from the
kittycats' curiosity.

Karen invented pussycat games. The cats hopped
and jumped, trying to catch the flashlight's beam.
They scampered, pranced and dashed after tin
foil balls and pom-poms on a string. Then Karen
finished the afternoon with their favorite—a game
of catnip-mouse tag.

That evening, as Karen relaxed in the tub after her busy cat day, she thought about how much she missed her Mister Whiskers.

To take her mind off her own lost cat, she named the thirty-seven cats. She called them:

Swe

Midnight

Bug

Tank

Drifter

Patch

Spot

Marmalade

Oreo

Muffin

Bear

Flash

Goldie

Groucho

Domino

Boo

Shredder

Baxter
and Stripe

Dash

Purrcee

Café

Scooter

Pinky

Puff-Baby

Snowball

Blur

Clawdia

Marbles

Frizbee

Tux

Teddy

Ruggles

Shadow

Smudge

Scrap

Socks

That night as Karen slept, the cats drifted in to snuggle up on her bed. Covered with a heavy warm blanket of purring furriness, she had strange and magical cat dreams.

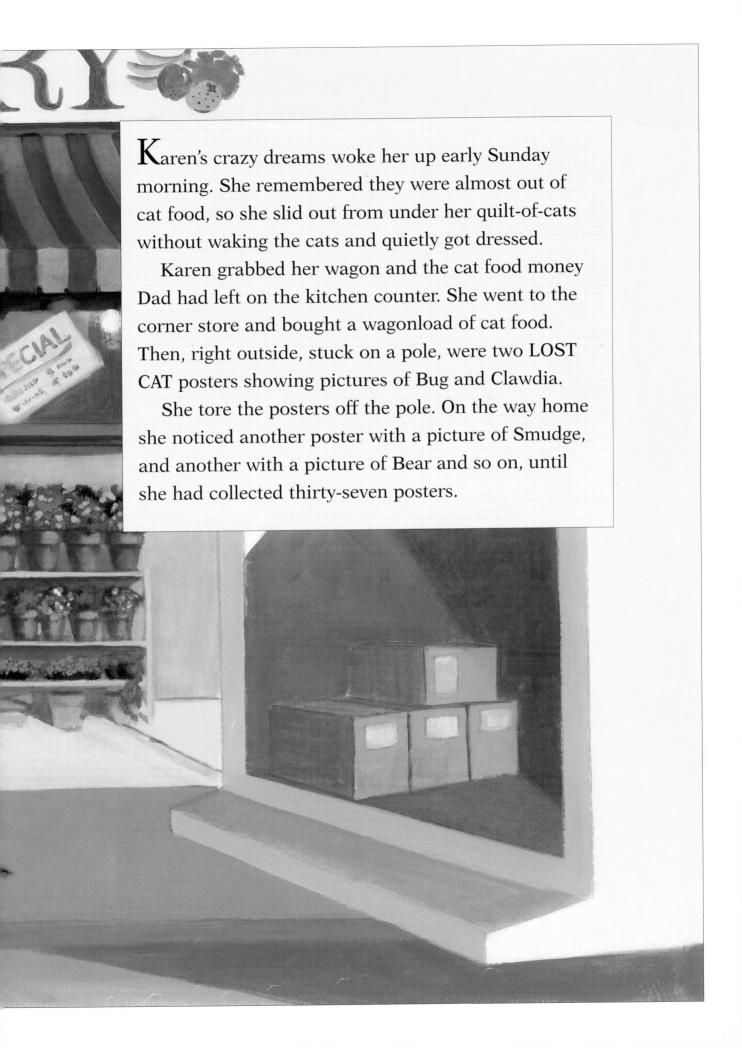

Karen's crazy dreams woke her up early Sunday morning. She remembered they were almost out of cat food, so she slid out from under her quilt-of-cats without waking the cats and quietly got dressed.

Karen grabbed her wagon and the cat food money Dad had left on the kitchen counter. She went to the corner store and bought a wagonload of cat food. Then, right outside, stuck on a pole, were two LOST CAT posters showing pictures of Bug and Clawdia.

She tore the posters off the pole. On the way home she noticed another poster with a picture of Smudge, and another with a picture of Bear and so on, until she had collected thirty-seven posters.

When she got home, she showed the posters to her parents. They rassled the cats into the car and took them to their real homes. At each stop Karen told the owners about their cat's adventures and apologized for borrowing their cats. She hugged each cat good-bye and kissed its furry little head.

Seeing the cats go back home made Karen miss them, but not as much as she missed her Mister Whiskers.

That night Karen sat at her window thinking about all those cats and their fun and commotion. Then she thought about Mister Whiskers. He had been lost now for two whole days.

Just then a familiar meow came through the window.

Karen ran down the stairs, opened the door and scooped up a cat.

"Mister Whiskers, you're back!" Karen laughed.

The End